Anubis: The History and Legacy of the Ancient Egyptian God of the Afterlife

By Markus Carabas and Charles River Editors

Jeff Dahl's depiction of Anubis

About Charles River Editors

Charles River Editors is a boutique digital publishing company, specializing in bringing history back to life with educational and engaging books on a wide range of topics. Keep up to date with our new and free offerings with this 5 second sign up on our weekly mailing list, and visit Our Kindle Author Page to see other recently published Kindle titles.

We make these books for you and always want to know our readers' opinions, so we encourage you to leave reviews and look forward to publishing new and exciting titles each week.

Introduction

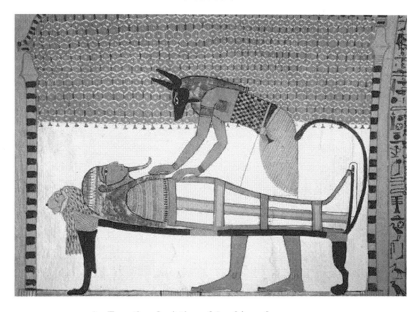

An Egyptian depiction of Anubis and a mummy

Anubis

"When Nephthys gave birth to Anubis, Isis treated the child as if it were her own; for Nephthys is that which is beneath the earth and invisible, Isis that which is above the earth and visible; and the circle which touches these, called the horizon, being common to both, has received the name Anubis, and is represented in form like a dog; for the dog can see with his eyes both by night and by day alike."[1]

Africa may have given rise to the first human beings, and Egypt probably gave rise to the first great civilizations, which continue to fascinate modern societies across the globe nearly 5,000 years later. From the Library and Lighthouse of Alexandria to the Great Pyramid at Giza, the Ancient Egyptians produced several wonders of the world, revolutionized architecture and construction, created some of the world's first systems of mathematics and medicine, and established language and art that spread across the known world. With world-famous leaders like King Tut and Cleopatra, it's no wonder that today's world has so many Egyptologists.

---

[1] Plutarch *On Isis and Osiris 14*

What makes the accomplishments of the Ancient Egyptians all the more remarkable is that Egypt was historically a place of great political turbulence. Its position made it both valuable and vulnerable to tribes across the Mediterranean and the Middle East, and Ancient Egypt had no shortage of its own internecine warfare. Its most famous conquerors would come from Europe, with Alexander the Great laying the groundwork for the Hellenic Ptolemy line and the Romans extinguishing that line after defeating Cleopatra and driving her to suicide.

Perhaps the most intriguing aspect of ancient Egyptian civilization was its inception from the ground up, as the ancient Egyptians had no prior civilization which they could use as a template. In fact, ancient Egypt itself became a template for the civilizations that followed. The Greeks and the Romans were so impressed with Egyptian culture that they often attributed many attributes of their own culture–usually erroneously–to the Egyptians. With that said, some minor elements of ancient Egyptian culture were, indeed, passed on to later civilizations. Egyptian statuary appears to have had an initial influence on the Greek version, and the ancient Egyptian language continued long after the pharaonic period in the form of the Coptic language.

Although the Egyptians may not have passed their civilization directly on to later peoples, the key elements that comprised Egyptian civilization, including their religion, early ideas of state, and art and architecture, can be found among other civilizations. For instance, civilizations far separated in time and space, such as China and Mesoamerica, possessed key elements that were similar to those found in ancient Egypt. Indeed, since Egyptian civilization represented some fundamental human concepts, a study of their culture can be useful when trying to understand many other pre-modern cultures.

To the ancient Egyptians, as was the case with any society made up of inquiring humans, the world was a confusing and often terrifying place of destruction, death and unexplained phenomena. In order to make sense of such an existence, they resorted to teleological stories. Giving a phenomenon a story made it less horrifying, and it also helped them make sense of the world around them. Unsurprisingly, then, the ancient Egyptian gods permeated every aspect of existence.

Given the abundance of funerary artifacts that have been found within the sands of Egypt, it sometimes seems as though the Ancient Egyptians were more concerned with the matters of the afterlife than they were with matters of the life they experienced from day to day. This is underscored most prominently by the pyramids, which have captured the world's imagination for centuries.

Thus, it's little surprise that Anubis was one of the most important gods in the Egyptian pantheon. The image of Anubis, with his jet-black jackal's head downturned in merciless judgment, continues to inspire artists and neo-Pagans today. There is something about this somber figure that has made him stand the test of time and allowed him to survive while so many gods and goddesses have fallen from memory in the wake of newer religions that are aided by a more interconnected world. Perhaps it is because Anubis is associated with death, or maybe it's because the lack of references to him in Egypt's literary and archaeological record invites multiple interpretations. It also may be due to his appearances in the most emotive works of ancient Egyptian art, notably the vignettes from tombs depicting the mysterious journey of the dead, which beckon viewers to imagine an unearthly, poetic view of death so far removed from modern conceptions. In a sense, Anubis is both awful and majestic.

To the ancient Egyptians, however, Anubis evolved over millennia, and even though his image may strike fear into modern hearts, in ancient times, his appearance was somewhat comforting to those who feared the invisible spirits inhabiting all things beside the Nile. Just as the dog is today a figure of protection against violence and trespass, so too was Anubis a figure whose fearsome aspect was a source of comfort for those following the code of their religion, ensuring their piety would be defendable in the Hall of Justice at the end of their lives. How his image was taken up by later cultures, ones who were not acolytes of the ancient Egyptian religion, is fascinating and a testament to human imagination.

Anubis: The History and Legacy of the Ancient Egyptian God of the Afterlife looks at the god that had such a decisive impact on the Egyptians' concepts of death and afterlife. Along with pictures depicting important people, places, and events, you will learn about Anubis like never before.

Note

The absolute dating of individual pharaohs has been a matter of long debate among Egyptologists, mostly due to the existence of several king lists that vary in the number of years they assign to each ruler.

The basic outline comes from Manetho, one of two priestly advisors to Ptolemy I (305-282 BCE). Manetho's *History* divides the pharaohs into 30 native dynasties and gives the number of years each ruler was on the throne, but no complete copy of Manetho's work exists.

Other king lists are also fragmentary. The Palermo Stone from Dynasty V (2498-2345 BCE) is a fairly complete list starting from the last Predynastic kings, but it sadly ends in the middle of Dynasty V. The Royal List of Karnak goes all the way to Tuthmosis III (1504-1450 BCE) and is especially useful in that it records many of the minor rulers of the Second Intermediate Period, when Egypt was divided into two or more states. The Royal List of Abydos skips these kings but runs all the way to the reign of Seti I (1291-1278 BCE). The Royal Canon of Turin is a badly damaged papyrus dating to around 1200 BCE that gives the precise length of reign of each ruler, often down to the day. Many portions of the list are missing, however.

Discoveries of other texts and radiocarbon dating have helped refine the dates, but there are still competing theories regarding the chronology, and all have both merits and problems. For the sake of consistency, this work uses the chronology set forth by Egyptologist Peter A. Clayton in his various works. The reader should note that while Clayton's chronology is a popular one, it is by no means universally accepted.

The Origins of Ancient Egyptian Mythology

Ancient Egypt spans a history of some 3,000 years, depending on how people want to divide it up. Many cultures, such as ancient Greece, divided their lengthy histories either according to cultural changes, such as the "Classical Era" beginning with the onset of democracy and ending with the death of Alexander the Great, or by following the reigns of each subsequent ruler. In ancient Egypt, the vast history was originally divided into dynasties. Living in the 3rd century BCE, the Egyptian priest Manetho divided history into 30 dynasties, which later Egyptologists have grouped into longer periods according to how much of what is considered Egypt today fell under the rule of each king. They are given as follows, according to Shaw's chronology:[2]

The Pharaonic Period

Early Dynastic Period (Dynasties 1-2) ca.3050-2660 BCE

Old Kingdom (Dynasties 3-6) ca. 2660-2190 BCE

---

[2] Shaw 2015

First Intermediate Period (Dynasties 7-11) ca. 2190-2066 BCE

Middle Kingdom (Dynasties 11-12) ca. 2066-1780 BCE

Second Intermediate Period (Dynasties 13-17) ca. 1780-1549 BCE

New Kingdom (Dynasties 18-20) ca. 1549-1069 BCE

Third Intermediate Period (21-25) ca. 1069-664 BCE

Late Period (Dynasties 26-31) ca. 664-332 BCE

The Ptolemaic Period 332-30 BCE

The Roman Period 30 BCE – 395 CE

In order to understand why modern scholars chose to divide history into longer periods of dynastic rule, it is necessary to understand the geography of Egypt's ruled dominions. The river that defined and dictated much of ancient people's lives and ideologies, the Nile, runs from south to north, with a sprawling delta in the north and more barren land to the south. This distinction is the reason for one of the most confusing aspects of Egyptian history, as the "Upper Kingdom" was in the south and the "Lower Kingdom" was in the north.[3] These "Two Lands" were represented by two distinct crowns – the "Red Crown" for the Lower Kingdom and the "White Crown" for the "Upper Kingdom" – each worn by their distinct rulers and worn as a "Double Crown" when both kingdoms were unified. It was during the "intermediate" periods that the country was divided into the two kingdoms, and these periods were often marked by political turmoil and a distinct drop in cultural production, such as art and architecture.

From as early as the Early Dynastic Period, the country was divided into smaller dominions along the river that modern scholars call "Nomes." The word "nome" comes from the ancient Greeks who, during the rule of the Greek Ptolemaic dynasty (332-30 BCE) in Egypt, referred to each as a kind of "pasturage" coming under the overarching rule of the Pharaoh of that kingdom. This made for a useful way of organising the inhabitants of the two kingdoms, but it causes problems when trying to define what version of a common myth is the "correct" or "most widely believed." The reason for this is that the myths, though they had some similarities, could diverge widely from nome to nome. That is why writers such as the ancient historian Plutarch chose to single out a particular version of a myth and record or study it alone.

Later scholars further subdivided these various types of myth according to the cult center that either produced or "standardized" them.[4] They refer to them as "theologies," such as the "Memphite Theology" (myths from Memphis) or the "Heliopolitan Theology" (myths from

---

[3] Shaw 2015
[4] Shaw 2015

Heliopolis). There is the theory that these "theologies" were competing in some way with others from different cult centers. Shaw, however, takes the view that they were more alternatives than opposing theories and although each cult center would substitute a god from another nome for one of their own local deities, there wasn't really any kind of animosity between the differing believers. Despite the fact that there was no externally enforced dogma over the whole of Egypt, the Egyptians still managed to maintain some overarching concepts. One such concept is that of the creation of the universe. Generally speaking, there was a limitless dark ocean of "chaos" called Nun, out of which a god was born who instigated creation.[5] The different cult centers felt at liberty to amend or augment that concept to incorporate local tastes and allegiances to deities. Later on, during the period of the New Kingdom, the cult center of Thebes gained prominence and the priests there tried to unify the earlier traditions of Egypt. In this attempt, Amun was the creator god but the Thebans also incorporated the traditions of the major cult centers like Hermopolis, Memphis and Heliopolis, which often seem quite disparate accounts to the modern reader but were quite ingeniously brought together at Thebes around 1200 BCE.[6]

The general creation story contains within it two aspects that are crucial to understanding all of the myths of ancient Egypt: *maat* and *isfet*. Isfet represents chaos or disorder, generally speaking, and it was seen as a fundamental element of everything in existence. There was no notion of trying to eradicate isfet from their general lives in ancient Egypt; after all, it was said to be one of the elements that was present in the limitless ocean at the dawn of creation. The only desire for ancient Egyptians was that isfet never became more prevalent than maat, its opposite: justice. Maat was often depicted as a goddess wearing a feather on her head, which was also the hieroglyph that represented her.[7] She, or simply the concept of justice, was believed to be present in all aspects of life and if it was broken by anyone, there would be a punishment. According to the Middle Kingdom "Coffin Text" it was believed that Atum, the "Great Finisher" of creation,[8] inhaled maat in order to gain his consciousness: "Inhale your daughter Maat [said Nun to Atum] and raise her to your nostril so that your consciousness may live. May they not be far from you, your daughter Maat and your son Shu, whose name is "life" … it is your son Shu who will lift you up."[9]

After that, Atum was capable of making the waters of Nun recede away from him, making him rise above them and become "what remained" or the "mound of creation." It's important to take note of the fact that there was no creation until Atum inhaled life and justice. Therefore without maat and her dualistic counterpart, there would have been no world, and that is the reason for maat and isfet's ubiquity, as well as the acceptance of chaos in the world as seen by the ancient Egyptians. After Atum had separated himself from Nun, the children he kept inside, notably Shu

---

[5] Shaw 2015
[6] Shaw 2015
[7] Shaw 2015
[8] Shaw 2015
[9] 80 see Shaw 2015

and maat/isfet, often represented as a form of the goddess Tefnut, were now separated from their father, and Tefnut would go on to become the mother of all the gods.

The Recording of The Myths

Since each of the nomes had their own version of a given myth, collecting Egyptian myths into a definitive text was never possible. This has further exacerbated the mythologist's job, since these stories have survived in disparate versions and media.

The myths may have arrived at the hands of scholars from inscriptions on pyramid walls (such as the Old Kingdom's "Pyramid Texts"), painted on the inside of coffins (such as the Middle Kingdom's "Coffin Texts"), or texts written on papyri (such as the famous "Book of the Dead," which dates back to the Second Intermediate Period).[10] The mythologist's job is made even more exacting by the fact that, since the scribes who documented the myths assumed their readers were knowledgeable about the stories' details, they opted to refer to myths obliquely out of a sense of decorum. This was often the case for Osiris, whose death was a troublesome topic for those inscribing on the funerary monuments since it was thought that simply mentioning his death could "magically harm the deceased."[11]

---

[10] Shaw 2015
[11] Shaw 2015

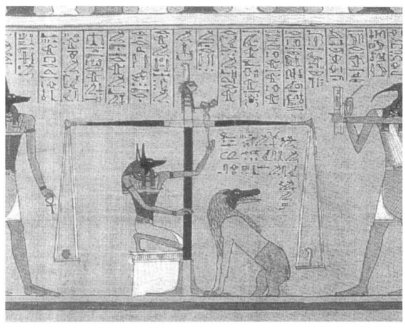

Scenes from the Book of the Dead

The vast history of Egypt makes tracking the development of certain myths a complex process. In terms of the oldest description of death, modern scholars have the Pyramid Texts. These were initially inscribed on the walls of the 5th Dynasty pyramid of Unas at Saqqara,[12] and they documented and gave advice to the king on his journey into the afterlife. These inscriptions were later copied onto other pyramids from the Old Kingdom and have therefore survived in good

---

[12] Shaw 2015

condition.

Unas Pyramid Text

Possibly the next most influential source came from the Roman era. Plutarch was a Greek historian and priest who lived in the late 1st and early 2nd century CE. He traveled to Egypt, it seems, but once he arrived there he was incapable of reading any hieroglyphs, so he largely depended on conversations with the locals and also a smattering of earlier literature that speculated on the identity of Egyptian gods and compared them with the Greeks' own pantheon. For instance, to the ancient Greeks the god Amun was Zeus, and the same applied to Hermes and Thoth, Apollo and Horus, and Dionysus and Osiris. The connection between Greece and Egypt was an ancient one and continues to have an influence on modern readers since many of the cult centers of ancient Egypt are referred to by their ancient Greek names, such as Hermopolis the City of Hermes, rather than their ancient Egyptian names, most likely because of the troublesome nature of transliterating Egyptian words. Nevertheless, Plutarch's *On Isis and Osiris* is the fullest account of the key myth in Egyptian mythology and is the best-known version for modern scholarship too.[13]

Despite the fact that Plutarch's account is late in terms of the wider history of Egyptian mythology, it is a surprisingly accurate take on the formation of the myth of Isis and Osiris,

---

[13] Pinch 2001

dating back to around 600 years before his arrival.[14] Of course, this does not make it an accurate account of the much earlier story of Osiris, but since describing his death and dismemberment was not a taboo for a Greek, his later account did not suffer from the obliqueness of the early sources.

Moreover, although Plutarch was not an Egyptian, he was an excellent scholar of foreign mythology. For him, the reason for writing down the myth of Isis and Osiris was to try and find a "fundamental truth" to the myths of both his own culture (of which he was a priest at Delphi for the remaining 30 years of his life) and that of his neighboring culture, which all Greeks considered to be much more ancient than their own. It was his scholarly approach and earnest desire to record the "truth" that makes his already interesting story worthy of study as a genuine account of the myth of Isis and Osiris.

---

[14] ibid.

A bust of Plutarch

The Gods as Concepts

Like in many polytheistic religious beliefs, the gods of ancient Egypt were neither omnipotent nor omnipresent, despite appearing in many locations simultaneously in some of the myths.[15] In fact, the ancient Egyptians used to worship the deity of the location they found themselves in, since each deity was more or less "present" in each part of the country. They were decidedly human in their relationships with each other. Just like the ancient Greek gods, they fought and argued, made love and married, and were ultimately capable of death, even if this meant that they would simply be reborn later on. Each god and goddess was "responsible" for an aspect of reality the ancient Egyptians encountered every day but, when they needed to, they could share their powers with another deity, which resulted in a kind of *merging* of the two. This was the case for the "dying sun god" who merged with Osiris so as to borrow his regenerative power and be "reborn" the following day.[16]

In the Memphite theology, the universe is created by the god Ptah, who "conceived the elements of creation in his heart and pronounced them into existence with the divine words as he pronounced their names." Yet some scholars believe that Ptah was only capable of such creation after he borrowed the heart and tongue from Amun, the ultimate creator; as such it was Ptah's being the personification of "creative process" that directed and guided Amun's creative abilities.[17]

When the deities merged or even appeared to take on the attributes of another god or goddess they were said to "literally become" the other deity. Shaw gives the example of Hathor attacking mankind with such a rage that she actually transformed into the bloodthirsty goddess Sekhmet. It might be best to think of the deities of ancient Egypt as manifestations rather than distinct personalities with concrete biographies. As such they helped the ancient Egyptians describe the world around them and, by giving precedents in their myths, explain away the more confusing aspects of why the world is the way it is.[18]

In ancient Egyptian culture the duality of deities – most often manifested in their male/female relationships – was an integral aspect of the belief system. This duality appeared in Nun, the limitless ocean of potentiality out of which the universe was born. Within those waters, the male and female aspects appeared as frogs (males) and snakes (females). There were four couples, according to the beliefs at Hermopolis, making up the eight most important gods of "pre-creation" referred to at this cult center as the "Ogdoad." Each of these gods and goddesses acquired names and, as a unit, they represented the earliest aspects of reality. Nun and Naunet

---

[15] Shaw 2015
[16] Shaw 2015
[17] Shaw 2015
[18] Shaw 2015

represented the "limitless waters" out of which everything was created; Huh and Hauhet represented the concept of "infinity"; Kuk and Kauket represented "darkness," and Amun and Amunet represented the concept of "hiddenness."[19] Later assessments of the Ogdoad, certainly by the time of the Theban attempt at "unification," emphasize the role of Amun in the creation of the first island and subsequently of the egg from which the sun god is hatched.

Atum's children, Shu and Tefnut, were also both siblings and a couple at the same time but their separation from their father led to the separation between an "above" and "below" by Shu, which created all of the space in which life could appear and grow. Also, Shu represented *neheh*, which was the Egyptian concept of cyclical time, whereas his wife came to represent *djet*, which was the concept of "time at a standstill, covering everything that is remaining and lasting, such as mummies or stone architecture," according to Gary Shaw.[20]

After Shu and Tefnut were separated from their father, they gave birth to a pair of deities called Nut and Geb. Nut was the sky goddess, often depicted as a naked lady with her hands and feet touching the earth and her body representing the heavens. Geb was the male earth god, usually represented as a reclining man with green skin with foliage on it. There is a story told in Plutarch's *Moralia* that equates the Egyptian gods with those of the ancient Greeks, and the story talks about how Nut and Geb (whom Plutarch equates with Greek deities Rhea and Cronus) can't make love because Shu kept them separated. When they tried to meet in secret, they incurred the wrath of the sun, or "Re." "They say that the Sun, when he became aware of Rhea's intercourse with Cronus, invoked a curse upon her that she should not give birth to a child in any month or year; but Hermes [Thoth], being enamoured of the [Moon], consorted with her. Later, playing at draughts with the moon, he won from her the seventieth part of each of her periods of illumination, and from all the winnings he composed five days, and intercalated them as an addition to the ['original'] three hundred and sixty days. The Egyptians even now call these five days intercalated and celebrate them as the birthdays of the gods. They relate that on the first of these days Osiris was born, and at the hour of his birth a voice issued forth saying, 'The Lord of All advances to the light.' However, some relate that a certain Pamyles, while he was drawing water in Thebes, heard a voice issuing from the shrine of Zeus, which bade him proclaim with a loud voice that a mighty and beneficent king, Osiris, had been born; and for this Cronus entrusted to him the child Osiris, which he brought up. It is in his honour that the festival of Pamylia is celebrated, a festival which resembles the phallic processions. On the second of these days Arueris was born whom they call Apollo, and some call him also the elder Horus. On the third day Typhon [Seth] was born, but not in due season or manner, but with a blow he broke through his mother's side and leapt [sic] forth. On the fourth day Isis was born in the regions that are ever moist; and on the fifth Nephthys, to whom they give the name of Finality and the name of Aphrodite, and some also the name of Victory. There is also a tradition that Osiris and Arueris were sprung from the Sun, Isis from Hermes, and [Seth] and Nephthys from Cronus. For this

[19] Shaw 2015
[20] Shaw 2015

reason the kings considered the third of the intercalated days as inauspicious, and transacted no business on that day, nor did they give any attention to their bodies until nightfall. They relate, moreover, that Nephthys became the wife of [Seth]; but Isis and Osiris were enamoured of each other and consorted together in the darkness of the womb before their birth. Some say that Arueris came from this union and was called the elder Horus by the Egyptians, but Apollo by the Greeks."[21]

Since many non-Greek sources do not include the birth of Horus the Elder in their lists counting all of Amun's children (Atum, Shu, Tefnut, Geb, Nut, Osiris, Seth, Isis, and Nephthys) the remaining nine make up what is known as the *Great Ennead*, deities who "represented the physical creation of the world."[22] That Amun was the Ennead's progenitor does not go far enough toward defining the power he maintained after their birth. It's important to remember that Amun created Atum, and then they became one deity that subsequently birthed all of existence, including the Ennead. For this reason, the ancient Egyptians saw Amun in all things, especially the gods and goddesses of the Ennead, who were understood to be forces called *Netjeru* (the "gods") that interacted independently but were always a part of Amun, the creator.

---

[21] On Isis and Osiris 12
[22] Shaw 2015

Anubis' Background

An Anubis mask

Genealogies of the gods are sources of entertainment for many interested in mythology. In the case of the ancient Greek religion, genealogy can reveal the character of child and parent in such a way that their family tree becomes a rich tapestry of complex relationships and characteristics. The sons of Ares have names - Phobos (fear) and Deimos (terror) - denoting aspects of war with which anyone who has experienced war would identify. In the case of ancient Egyptian genealogies, however, antiquity has blurred the lines to the point that such abstraction is difficult.

Sources from the First Intermediate Period describe Anubis as being either the son of Ra or the son of Hesat, a cow-headed goddess who suckled the pharaoh and gave life-giving milk to humankind. The connection with Hesat and Anubis seems odd at first, but when she is connected with Isis, the story takes on a little more detail. A truly odd parentage that also comes out of the First Intermediate Period is that of Bast or Bastet, the cat-headed goddess of ancient Egypt. To the modern reader, a dog being born from a cat may seem like the makings of a Saturday morning cartoon, rather than theology. There is, however, some method to this madness since Bast was also the goddess of perfume, which was kept in jars similar to the ointments used in the process of mummification, which is very much Anubis' realm. There are conflicting stories about whether Bast was Anubis' mother or wife at the time, but either way, the association reveals his connection with mummification and death from an early time.

It is from the Roman period that the most rounded, fullest account of Anubis' parentage comes to light. Plutarch traveled to Egypt, it seems, but once he arrived he was incapable of reading any hieroglyphs, so he largely depended on the testimonies of locals and a smattering of earlier literature speculating on the identity of Egyptian gods, usually by comparing them with the Greek pantheon. For instance, to the ancient Greeks, the god Amun was Zeus, and the same went for Hermes and Thoth, Apollo and Horus, and Dionysus and Osiris. The connection between Greece and Egypt was an ancient one that continues to have an influence on modern readers since many of Egypt's cult centers are referred to by their ancient Greek names (such as Hermopolis, the City of Hermes) rather than their ancient Egyptian names, most likely due to the troublesome nature of transliterating Egyptian words. Nevertheless, Plutarch's *On Isis and Osiris* is the fullest account of the key myth in Egyptian mythology and is considered the best-known version with respect to modern scholarship.[23]

Despite the fact that Plutarch's account is "late" in terms of the wider history of Egyptian mythology, it is a surprisingly accurate take on the formation of the myth of Isis and Osiris dating back to around 600 years before his arrival.[24] This does not, of course, make it an accurate account of the much earlier story of Osiris, but since describing his death and dismemberment was not a taboo for the Greek priest, his later account did not suffer the obliqueness of the early sources. Although Plutarch was not an Egyptian, he was an avid scholar of foreign mythology, and it was his scholarly approach and earnest desire to record the "truth" that made his already interesting story something worthy of study as a genuine account of the myth of Isis and Osiris.

Plutarch believed Isis was at the heart of this "universal truth," and his account of the birth of Anubis certainly highlights her magnanimity and generosity. He refers to his conversations with local Egyptian priests on the matter in *On Isis and Osiris*: "They relate also that Isis, learning that Osiris in his love had consorted with her sister through ignorance, in the belief that she was Isis, and seeing the proof of this in the garland of melilote [sic] which he had left with Nephthys, sought to find the child; for the mother, immediately after its birth, had exposed it because of her fear of Typhon. And when the child had been found, after great toil and trouble, with the help of dogs which led Isis to it, it was brought up and became her guardian and attendant, receiving the name of Anubis, and it is said to protect the gods just as dogs protect men."[25]

---

[23] Pinch 2001
[24] ibid.
[25] Plutarch *On Isis and Osiris* 14

Here, Anubis' role as the guardian is brought to light. It is very likely that Anubis, the watcher of the dead and tombs, was an influence to Plutarch when he wrote this passage, but it is not until much later in the text that Plutarch amplifies the story with further details about who this "guide of souls" was: "When Nephthys gave birth to Anubis, Isis treated the child as if it were her own; for Nephthys is that which is beneath the earth and invisible, Isis that which is above the earth and visible; and the circle which touches these, called the horizon, being common to both, has received the name Anubis, and is represented in form like a dog; for the dog can see with his eyes both by night and by day alike. And among Egyptians Anubis is thought to possess this faculty, which is similar to that which Hecate is thought to possess among the Greeks, for Anubis is a deity of the lower world as well as a god of Olympus. Some are of the opinion that Anubis is Cronus. For this reason, inasmuch as he generates all things out of himself and conceives all things within himself, he has gained the appellation of "Dog." There is, therefore, a certain mystery observed by those who revere Anubis; in ancient times the dog obtained the highest honours in Egypt; but, when Cambyses had slain the Apis and cast him forth, nothing came near the body or ate of it save only the dog; and thereby the dog lost his primacy and his place of honour above that of all the other animals."[26]

The description of Isis being "above the earth" and Nephthys being "below" it, sharing a son as they shared the horizon between the two, gives the reader a hint at the seed which will germinate into the role of Anubis in alchemical and hermetic texts into the Renaissance. Regarding the point that the ancient Egyptians revered dogs, Plutarch was most certainly correct, and this is made clear in the naming of the home of Anubis as the City of Dogs.

In ancient Egyptian religion, each of the Nomes worshiped a greater collective of gods but gave especial prominence to one deity in particular. Anubis took precedence in the 17th Nome of Upper Egypt, and it was at the city of Cynopolis - the City of Dogs - that Anubis was particularly important. The name is Greek and was given to the Egyptian city much later, but there was a cemetery for dogs in the city and the worship of Anubis was very well attested, so the nomenclature made sense.

It was the custom of many Greeks and Romans to wander around the mystical land of Egypt, quizzing the locals on their much older religious practices. Plutarch was one such wanderer, and he recorded a curious religious rivalry between Cynopolis and the nearby city of Oxyrhynchus: "And in my day the people of Oxyrhynchus caught a dog and sacrificed it and ate it up as if it had been sacrificial meat, because the people of Cynopolis were eating fish known as the Oxyrhynchus or pike. As a result of this they became involved in war and inflicted much harm upon each other; and later they were both brought to order through chastisement by the Romans."[27]

---

[26] Plutarch *On Isis and Osiris* 44
[27] Plutarch Isis And Osiris 72

Anubis' Roles

Anubis' association with the dog, or the African Golden Wolf to be more specific, came as a result of ritual burial practices at the time. Anubis is most often depicted as either wandering around graveyards or sitting in an elevated position above the burial sites over which he watched. As a "dog," he was a sentinel, but he garnered the animalistic form from the fact that ancient Egyptian graveyards were often populated by "dogs" that would dig up those who were shallowly buried and make a nocturnal feast of them. It's surprising that Anubis was not a hated figure for this reason, but perhaps the very fact they were seen roaming the area led the ancient Egyptians to believe their intentions were honorable, or at very least sanctioned by the gods. However it happened, Anubis acquired the role of sentinel of tombs.

In ancient Egyptian religion, there are two deities inherently associated with death and the Duat, the land of the dead. These were Anubis and Osiris. The reason for their association is more a question of chronology than shared duties. By the Middle Kingdom, Anubis had become the god of mummification and the protector of tombs and cemeteries. Osiris was the King of the Dead, but this was not always the case. Originally, Anubis was the Lord of the Dead, but his position was usurped by Osiris.

Prior to the Middle Kingdom, it is likely that Osiris was a vegetation god, obscure and of little importance, but by the end of the Old Kingdom, Osiris ceased being the god helping only kings gain life after death. Instead, the Egyptians came to believe Osiris could offer everlasting life to all,[28] and since the afterlife was now so crucial to everyone, Anubis came to represent the most obvious, starkest aspects of death known by the average Egyptian: the cemetery and the fate of the people who became fodder for the "the dog who swallowed millions."

Osiris is most often the protagonist because his story is the only myth to eventually garner more fame than that of his son, Horus, and his brother, Seth. The tale of Osiris begins when his father, Ra, grows weary of humanity and decides to leave them to their own devices while he lives out the rest of eternity amongst the stars. He leaves his "magic" behind in the form of snakes. Before he became the king of humans and gods, however, Osiris wished to "sow his royal oats" on a trip of truly Bacchic proportion: "Now after Osiris had established the affairs of Egypt and turned the supreme power over to Isis his wife, they say that he placed Hermes at her side as counsellor because his prudence raised him above the king's other friends, and as general of all the land under his sway he left Heracles, who was both his kinsman and renowned for his valour and physical strength…then he himself left Egypt with his army to make his campaign, taking in his company also his brother, whom the Greeks call Apollo. And it was Apollo, they say, who discovered the laurel, a garland of which all men place about the head of this god above all others. The discovery of ivy is also attributed to Osiris by the Egyptians and made sacred to this god, just as the Greeks also do in the case of Dionysus. And in the Egyptian language, they

---

[28] Tyldesley 2011

say, the ivy is called the "plant of Osiris" and for purposes of dedication is preferred to the vine, since the latter sheds its leaves while the former ever remains green; the same rule, moreover, the ancients have followed in the case of other plants also which are perennially green, ascribing, for instance, the myrtle to Aphrodite and the laurel to Apollo."[29]

After this episode, Osiris meets with Dionysus' favorite mythological beings, the satyrs and muses. Before returning home to Egypt with a plethora of gifts, Osiris spends his time merrymaking in full Dionysian style and giving technology and power to foreign peoples so that they will eventually pay tribute to him. As Plutarch put it, "One of the first acts related [to] Osiris in his reign was to deliver the Egyptians from their destitute and brutish manner of living. This he did by showing them the fruits of cultivation, by giving them laws, and by teaching them to honour the gods. Later he travelled over the whole earth civilizing it without the slightest need of arms, but most of the peoples he won over to his way by the charm of his persuasive discourse combined with song and all manner of music. Hence the Greeks came to identify him with Dionysus."[30]

It was understood that Osiris' son, Anubis, joined him on this adventure, though the sober, canine-headed god barely appears in the tales of Osiris' debauchery.[31] Little did father or son know that the second son, Seth, was plotting to usurp the throne of Ra while his brother and nephew were out gallivanting and ingratiating themselves with the people of Egypt and abroad:

> "During his absence the tradition is that [Seth] attempted nothing revolutionary because Isis, who was in control, was vigilant and alert; but when [Osiris] returned home [Seth] contrived a treacherous plot against him and formed a group of conspirators seventy-two in number. He had also the co-operation of a queen from Ethiopia who was there at the time and whose name they report as Aso. [Seth], having secretly measured Osiris's [sic] body and having made ready a beautiful chest of corresponding size artistically ornamented, caused it to be brought into the room where the festivity was in progress. The company was much pleased at the sight of it and admired it greatly, whereupon [Seth] jestingly promised to present it to the man who should find the chest to be exactly his length when he lay down in it. They all tried it in turn, but no one fitted it; then Osiris got into it and lay down, and those who were in the plot ran to it and slammed down the lid, which they fastened by nails from the outside and also by using molten lead. Then they carried the chest to the river and sent it on its way to the sea through the Tanitic Mouth. Wherefore the Egyptians even to this day name this mouth the hateful and execrable. Such is the tradition…

[29] Library of History 17
[30] On Isis and Osiris 1.13
[31] Shaw 2015

"The first to learn of the deed and to bring to men's knowledge an account of what had been done were the Pans and Satyrs who lived in the region around Chemmis, and so, even to this day, the sudden confusion and consternation of a crowd is called a panic. Isis, when the tidings reached her, at once cut off one of her tresses and put on a garment of mourning in a place where the city still bears the name of Kopto. Others think that the name means deprivation, for they also express "deprive" by means of "*koptein*." But Isis wandered everywhere at her wits' end; no one whom she approached did she fail to address, and even when she met some little children she asked them about the chest. As it happened, they had seen it, and they told her the mouth of the river through which the friends of [Seth] had launched the coffin into the sea. Wherefore the Egyptians think that little children possess the power of prophecy, and they try to divine the future from the portents which they find in children's words, especially when children are playing about in holy places and crying out whatever chances to come into their minds.

"As they relate, Isis proceeded to her son Horus, who was being reared in Buto, and bestowed the chest in a place well out of the way; but [Seth], who was hunting by night in the light of the moon, happened upon it. Recognizing the body he divided it into fourteen parts and scattered them, each in a different place. Isis learned of this and sought for them again, sailing through the swamps in a boat of papyrus. This is the reason why people sailing in such boats are not harmed by the crocodiles, since these creatures in their own way show either their fear or their reverence for the goddess.

"The traditional result of Osiris's [sic] dismemberment is that there are many so-called tombs of Osiris in Egypt; for Isis held a funeral for each part when she had found it. Others deny this and assert that she caused effigies of him to be made and these she distributed among the several cities, pretending that she was giving them his body, in order that he might receive divine honours in a greater number of cities...and also that, if [Seth] should succeed in overpowering Horus, he might despair of ever finding the true tomb when so many were pointed out to him, all of them called the tomb of Osiris.

"Of the parts of Osiris's [sic] body the only one which Isis did not find was the male member, for the reason that this had been at once tossed into the river, and the lepidotus, the sea-bream, and the pike had fed upon it; and it is from these very fishes the Egyptians are most scrupulous in abstaining. But Isis made a replica of the member to take its place, and consecrated the phallus, in honour of which the Egyptians even at the present day celebrate a festival. [32]

---

[32] Plutarch *On Isis and Osiris 13-16*

Stories of Anubis preparing Osiris' body were fairly common throughout the Nomes of Egypt, and they invariably included Seth attempting to foil the process and ensure the "permanent" death of his brother and adversary. It is here that Anubis earns his not-so-coveted role of "mummifier" and protector of the gods. In the "Jumilhac Papyrus," which dates to the time of the Ptolemies or Romans, a story is recorded in which Seth tries to attack the body of Osiris in the form of a leopard. Anubis, who was protecting Osiris' body, was as watchful as a guard dog, and he caught Seth in the process and speckled his hide with a hot brand before subsequently flaying him and wearing the spotted hide. This is a clear etiological myth, both for how the leopard came to be a spotted animal and for how priests came to wear leopard skins during burials.[33]

There is another story of the watchful Anubis thwarting Seth's plans, described with exquisite brevity by acclaimed historian Gary Shaw: "One day, when it was approaching twilight, Seth discovered the time that Anubis would leave Osiris' body alone in the wabet (the place of embalming). To evade detection, the trickster god transformed himself into Anubis and, just as planned, the guards failed to recognize him. Snatching Osiris' body from within the wabet, he sailed away on the river, carrying the corpse westward. But Anubis soon learned what had transpired and, along with the gods of his entourage, set off in pursuit. When they met, Seth took the form of a bull to intimidate the dog-faced god, but Anubis caught and tied Seth by the arms and legs, and severed his phallus and testicles. His enemy defeated, Anubis placed Osiris' body on his back, ready to return him to the wabet and imprisoned Seth in a place of torture at Saka, in the 17th Upper Egyptian Nome."[34]

There is another vivid story of Seth's clever plans to thwart Anubis' work, involving disguising himself as Anubis once more to trick the guards of Osiris' body. Seth was captured, and this time, he was forced to become the seat on which Osiris would sit for eternity.

Seth was understandably less than happy about the situation, and he eventually escaped to the desert, presumably to plot yet another attack on his brother's corpse, but Anubis had other plans. Anubis and god of magic, Thoth, chased Seth through the desert, and when they caught up with him, they used their magic to bring him down and bind his arms and legs. Tired of his incessant malevolence, Anubis and Thoth hung the bound god over a fire and burned him alive. The smell of burning flesh rose into the sky until it reached Ra and the others who made the ether their home.[35] When they decided Seth had been cooked enough, Anubis flayed the skin from his body again and wore it as a disguise. Then, he strode to the top of the mountain where Seth's loyal followers were lying in wait for their master's next diabolical plan, and Anubis feigned malevolence in their presence. When they finally fell asleep, with one swipe of his sword, Anubis decapitated them, leaving rivulets of blood trickling down the mountain.

---

[33] See Zandee 1960
[34] 2015
[35] see Shaw 2015

Whenever he had a minute away from flaying, burning, or otherwise defending Osiris' body from Seth, Anubis was creating and learning the craft of mummification. Even though the process of mummification was considered a sacred and magical event, the ancient Egyptians were not immune to the more macabre features of it. This is clear from another story about Anubis, taking place while he is in the *wabet*. They say that the sight of Osiris dead body—possibly rotting at this point but certainly reconstructed, at least—caused Anubis such horror, he simply had to share it with somebody. Rather than lose face among the gods or appear as if he were incapable of his duties, he turned himself into a legion of lizards, slipped out of the wabet through the cracks in the walls, and whispered the horrors to anybody he could. News finally reached the gods, and they wept for Osiris and Anubis.

Anubis completed his task, nevertheless, and in doing so, he became the inventor and god of mummification and Osiris became the first Egyptian mummy. After the mummification came the burial, and this was not without its perils, because Seth would not quit. At one point, he attacked the funeral procession, which consisted of a march of weeping and wailing gods and goddesses including Isis and Nephthys, with vile reptilian creatures that later turned into trampling cattle, but they were repelled by the mourning deities.[36] When it came to place Osiris' body in the ground, Anubis called upon those creatures left by Ra with Ra's magic inside them. Out of the ground, dozens of venomous snakes slithered into a protective circle around the funeral procession. Seth was unable to break through, and Osiris was laid to rest before he became the new Lord of the Dead.

Ancient Egyptian Burial Practices

In order to truly understand the tombs found across Egypt, especially the ones located in the Valley of the Kings, it is first necessary to understand the basics of Ancient Egyptian burial practices. "Burial" is the term commonly used to describe the collection of ancient Egyptian funerary rites that dealt with both death and the soul's journey on the way to the afterlife. A royal Egyptian burial would culminate with the placement of the deceased pharaoh's mummy in his tomb, often located within an elaborate complex.

Today, it is generally understood that the process of mummification came about after a lot of trial and error, as well as countless ritualistic revisions, so the stories of Seth's attacks and Anubis' sober protection were later inventions. By the 5th Dynasty, there is enough in the literary record to give modern historians a good idea of this evolution.

It seems there was a basic belief in the possibility of maintaining a corpse for eternity, and if so, permanent death could be averted, at least for the king. Initially, the hope of a future beyond death was not on offer to the general populace of ancient Egypt. It's unclear as to why, exactly, this was considered the case, but Joyce Tyldesley describes the king's capacity for "three

---

[36] ibid.

distinctive and ineffably complex spirits or souls which, trapped in his body during his lifetime, would be released at his death, allowing him to sail in the solar boat of Ra, dwell in the Field of Reeds or shine as an eternal star in the deep blue sky."[37]

No comprehensive description of these "spirits or souls" has yet been found in the literary or archaeological record, but historians like Tyldesley have managed to piece together a working model of what they were based on what has survived. The first is the *ba*. This is similar to the "ghost" of a person or god in that it represented the soul and personality of the dead king that "lived" within the tomb but was capable of visiting the land of the living. The second is the *ka,* which could be described as the deceased's "life-force," except that it was not as "permanent" as the soul might be described. In fact, the ka could cease to exist if the deceased's body had decomposed to the point where it no longer resembled the form it inhabited in the living world. The ka is fascinating in that every living thing was said to have a ka, but certain gods were capable of having more than one. Tyldesley gives the example of Atum in this respect: "As everything in existence could be traced back to the original creator Atum, everything in existence could, in theory, be classed as a ka of Atum."[38] The final aspect is the *akh*. This is the least understood of the three, but from the surviving art and literature, it is understood to be the aspect of immortality that could be achieved if the physical and spoken rituals were correctly performed on the deceased.

The actual process of mummification passed through many stages before it was more or less finalized in the Third Intermediate Period. It began by recognizing the sand-graves that desiccated the body while allowing the tissue to survive the rotting process. After this, a process similar to creating plaster casts came about, so the body rotted away, but the form of the deceased would survive and thus, hopefully, so would its ka. Over the centuries, salts and ointments were used to preserve the bodies that are now on display in museums throughout the world.

Mummification was an act of art and science with deep religious meaning and significance since the survival of the body was considered the only way to ensure a happy afterlife. Given the importance of the king in ancient Egypt, Anubis' role in giving humans the ability to preserve and ultimately raise the king beyond the realm of mere mortals to live eternally with the gods of all creation is a role that cannot be overstated, even if his appearance in the literary record is relatively scant.

Eventually, it was believed every Egyptian was destined for eternity after death, but the Egyptians had no conception of an ethereal, otherworldly afterlife. Instead, the Egyptians believed that they would spend eternity in an eternal Egypt and that their lives there would mirror a perfect reflection of life as it had been lived in the Egypt of this earth. Eternal Egypt was

---

[37] 2011
[38] ibid.

known to Ancient Egyptians by a few different names. Most commonly, it was known as The Field of Reeds, but it was also commonly called Lily Lake and the Field of Plenty. Egyptian burial rites reflected this vision of eternity.

Scholars have established that the first Egyptian burial rites were practiced by 4000 BCE, and from that point until the Roman takeover of Egypt around 30 BCE, Egyptian burial rites demonstrated an unwavering focus on eternal life and the continuance of personal existence after death.[39]

Egyptian burial rites were very dramatic, even though Egyptians hoped that the deceased would find eternal bliss in the Field of Reeds. The ancient Greek historian Herodotus describes these dramatic rites: "As regards mourning and funerals, when a distinguished man dies, all the women of the household plaster their heads and faces with mud, then, leaving the body indoors, perambulate the town with the dead man's relatives, their dresses fastened with a girdle, and beat their bared breasts. The men too, for their part, follow the same procedure, wearing a girdle and beating themselves like the women. The ceremony over, they take the body to be mummified."[40]

Mummification, by far the most well-known aspect of the Egyptian burial, was practiced in Egypt by the middle of the 3rd millennium BCE. Most scholars believe that mummification became common due to the way in which corpses were often preserved in Egypt's arid sands. At a very early point in the history of their civilizations, the Egyptians seem to have developed the concept of an eternal soul, and it was believed that the entire[41] body of the deceased needed to be preserved on Earth in order for that soul to be able to enjoy an eternal afterlife.

Once a person had died, his family would bring his body to the embalmers, where, as Herodotus explained, the professionals would "produce specimen models in wood, graded in quality. They ask which of the three [levels of service] is required, and the family of the dead, having agreed upon a price, leave the embalmers to their task…The best and most expensive model is said to represent [Osiris], the next best is somewhat inferior and cheaper while the third is cheapest of all."[42]

---

[39] The ancient world was fascinated by the Egyptian burial, which became well known via cultural transmission through trade along the Silk Road. The Egyptian buran doubtless bore a great influenced on a number of other civilizations and religions—it was certainly a major source of inspiration for the Christian vision of eternal life.

[40] (Nardo, 110)

[41] Ancient Egyptians believed that the soul consisted of nine separate parts. The physical body was known as the *Khat*; the *Ka* was one's double form; the *Ba* was a human headed bird aspect which was able to speed between earth and the heavens; *Shuyet* was the shadow self; *Akh* was the immortal, transformed self; *Sahu* and *Sechem* were aspects of the *Akh*; *Ab* was the heart, which was the source of good and evil; *Ren* was one's secret name. Without the *Ka* and the *Ba*, the *Khat* was believed to be unable to recognize itself.

[42] Ikram, 53; Nardo, 110. The three choices dictated not only what kind of coffin the deceased could be buried in, but also the funerary rites that would be available to him and the treatment of his body.

The ancient historian Ikram described the mummification procedure as follows: "The key ingredient in mummification was natron, or netjry, divine salt. It is a mixture of sodium bicarbonate, sodium carbonate, sodium sulphate and sodium chloride that occurs naturally in Egypt, most commonly in the Wadi Natrun some sixty-four kilometres northwest of Cairo. It has desiccating and defatting properties and was the preferred desiccant, although common salt was also used in more economical burials."[43]

In the most expensive form of burial, the deceased's brain was removed "via the nostrils with an iron hook, and what cannot be reached with the hook is washed out with drugs; next the flank is opened with a flint knife and the whole contents of the abdomen removed; the cavity is then thoroughly cleaned and washed out, firstly with palm wine and again with an infusion of ground spices. After that it is filled with pure myrrh, cassia, and every other aromatic substance, excepting frankincense, and sewn up again, after which the body is placed in natron, covered entirely over for seventy days – never longer. When this period is over, the body is washed and then wrapped from head to foot in linen cut into strips and smeared on the underside with gum, which is commonly used by the Egyptians instead of glue. In this condition the body is given back to the family who have a wooden case made, shaped like a human figure, into which it is put."[44]

---

[43] Ikram 55
[44] Ikram 54; a citation of Herodotus.

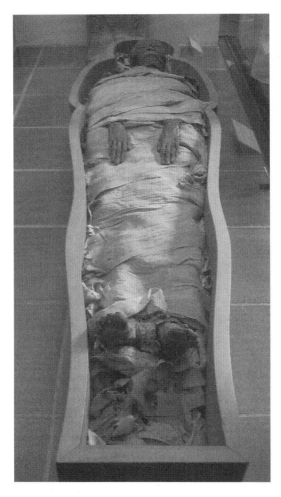

Joshua Sherurcij's picture of an Egyptian mummy

The third and cheapest method of embalming, according to Ikram, simply involved washing out the intestines and keeping the body for 70 days in natron.[45] While the internal organs were removed in order to help preserve the corpse, it was believed that the deceased would still need

---

[45] Ikram 54; a citation of Herodotus. Natron is a naturally occurring mixture of sodium carbonate decahydrate and sodium bicarbonate along with small quantities of sodium chloride and sodium sulfate.

them in the afterlife, so they were preserved separately and kept in canopic jars within the tomb.

Even those Egyptians who couldn't afford to pay anything at all were given some kind of burial, as it was believed that the souls of the deceased who had not been properly buried would return as a ghost and spend eternity haunting the living.[46] Even the basic kind of mummification could be extremely expensive, so the poor often took to giving their used clothing to the embalmers so that it could be used to wrap the corpse.[47]

Once the corpse had been mummified, it was time for the funeral. The Ancient Egyptians believed that the remembrance of the dead by the living ensured that the dead would continue to exist in the Field of Reeds. A great show of grief was thought to resound in the Hall of Truth (or Hall of Osiris)—the first major destination of the deceased in the afterlife. Thus, the funeral was both an occasion to mourn the loss of the deceased and an occasion to celebrate and honor his life. Regardless of how popular the deceased may have been in life, it was traditional to have a group of professional mourners, called Kites, accompanying the funeral procession and burial. The Kites were paid to lament loudly throughout these proceedings, and traditionally, they would sing the "Lamentation of Isis and Nephthys," a lamentation song that had its origins in the myth of the two goddesses weeping over the death of Osiris. The song of the Kites was meant to inspire the other mourners at the funeral to show their emotion.

At some point prior to the funeral procession or immediately before placing the mummy in the tomb, a priest would perform the Opening of the Mouth Ceremony. This ceremony underscored the importance of the physical body; its purpose was to reanimate the corpse so that the immortal

---

[46] The return of a ghost was considered to be a very serious matter, as the Egyptians were not able to tolerate the idea of non-existence. If the deceased was not given a proper burial (or if their loved ones had committed some sin before or after death), the gods gave the *Akh* dispensation to return to earth in order to redress the wrong. The Akh would then harass the living, who would have to plead their case to the ghost in the hopes of receiving a reasonable response. If they were not able to receive one themselves, a priest would have to intervene and serve as arbiter between the living and the dead. If, for example, misfortune were to befall a widower, that misfortune would first be attributed to some "sin" he had committed against his wife, who, omniscient in the Field of Reeds, was now punishing him. One such widower wrote a letter to his dead wife, begging her to leave him alone and insisting that he was innocent of any wrong-doing. The letter, which he delivered to her in her tomb, reads as follows: "What wicked thing have I done to you that I should have come to this evil pass? What have I done to you? But what you have done to me is to have laid hands on me although I had done nothing wicked to you. From the time I lived with you as your husband down to today, what have I done to you that I need hide? When you began to grow sick from the illness which you had, I caused a master-physician to be fetched...I spent eight months without eating and drinking like a man. I wept exceedingly together with my household in front of my street-quarter. I gave linen clothes to wrap you and left no benefit undone that had to be performed for you. And now, behold, I have spent three years alone without entering into a house, though it is not right that one like me should have to do it. This have I done for you sake. But, behold, you do not know good from bad." (Nardo, 32).

[47] Thus giving rise to the euphemistic phrase "the linen of yesterday" as a term for death which eventually came to be employed by the *Kites* (female professional mourners), who would lament that the deceased had once dressed in fine linens, but now slept in the linen of yesterday.

soul could continue to use it. In this ceremony, a priest recited spells while using a ritual blade to touch the mouth of the corpse—the touch of the blade was believed to enable the corpse to regain its ability to breathe, eat, and drink. Next, he touched the corpse's arms and legs so that it would be free to move about within the tomb (and beyond).

An Ancient Egyptian mural depicting the opening the mouth ceremony

A mural depicting the opening the mouth ceremony for King Tutankhamun

A depiction of Anubis on an ancient coffin from the New Kingdom

After the body was at last laid to rest, the tomb was sealed. Finally, the priest recited a number of other spells and prayers, usually the Litany of Osiris, and if the deceased was a pharaoh, the priest would recite a set of spells known as the Pyramid Text. With this recitation, the burial was complete, and the deceased was left to begin his journey to the Field of Reeds.

The Psychopomp

Jon Bodsworth's picture of a statuette of Anubis found in King Tut's tomb

The "psychopomp" is a Greek term for the common deity who guides the soul from the land of the living to the land of the dead. The word literally means "guide of souls," and it is a common role of some god or lesser deity in many religions. Azrael, Raven, Hermes, and Anubis are all examples of the deities that come to take the hand of the dead soul upon his or her passing and guide them toward their ultimate destiny.

Although each of these deities has their distinct characteristics, the similarities between Anubis and Hermes are particularly interesting. To see Anubis in this light, it is necessary to be familiar with the famous group of spells that became *The Book of the Dead*.

In the Pyramid of Unas in Giza, the burial chamber walls are covered in long vertical hieroglyphic inscriptions. Taken together, they are called the Pyramid Texts and include 283 different spells to help the soul make it to the land of the dead. The soul was required to prove its worthiness and respond correctly to a series of monstrous guardians before having its heart judged to see if the soul was worthy of making it to the next world. Some of these spells were apparently recited at various points during the burial ceremony. This in turn led to the Coffin Texts being developed later in the Middle Kingdom Period, and then *The Book of the Dead* from the New Kingdom era to the Ptolemaic Period.[48] This notion of magic inscriptions also played a part much later in history through pop culture's fixation on the idea that the pharaohs' mummies had curses. The idea that grave robbers and archaeologists suffered from these kinds of curses remains popular even today.[49]

Pyramid Texts in Unas' funerary chamber

According to *The Book of the Dead*, when someone dies and is mummified, they must depend on the knowledge they acquired in their lives to "survive" the perils of the Duat (the underworld or afterlife). This is fascinating, given the fact that modern concepts of the afterlife and its many

[48] Lehner, Mark. 1997. *The Complete Pyramids*. Thames and Hudson, Slovenia.
[49] Sommers, Stephen. 1999. *The Mummy*. Universal Pictures, USA.

forms often stress the importance of piety, honesty, and purity when approaching the challenges of what lies beyond. However, this was not the case in ancient Egypt, at least from the Middle Kingdom on.[50]

Once "beyond," the deceased had to use his or her knowledge of the spells in *The Book of the Dead* to negotiate a labyrinth of doorways, each with its own guardian that demanded the recitation of a set text before Anubis took him or her by the hand to lead them to the Hall of Justice, where there were 42 gods known as the "Assessors of Maat." Once there, the deceased greeted the "Lord of Justice" in another ritualized manner: "Hail to you, great god, Lord of Justice! I have come to you, my lord, that you may bring me so that I may see your beauty, for I know you and I know your name, and I know the names of the forty-two gods of those who are with you in this Hall of Justice, who live on those who cherish evil and who gulp down their blood on that day of the reckoning of the characters in the presence of Wennefer. Behold the double son of the Songstresses; Lord of Truth is your name. Behold, I have come to you, I have brought you truth, I have repelled falsehood for you. I have not done falsehood against men, I have no impoverished my associates, I have done no wrong in the Place of Truth, I have not learnt [sic] that which is not, I have done no evil, I have not daily made labour in excess of what was due to be done for me, my name has not reached the offices of those who control slaves, I have not deprived the orphan of his property, I have not done what the gods detest, I have not calumniated a servant to his master, I have not caused pain, I have not made hungry, I have not made to weep, I have not killed, I have not commanded to kill, I have not made suffering for anyone ... I am pure, pure, pure, pure! My purity is the purity of that great phoenix which is in Heracleopolis, because I am indeed the nose of the Lord of Wind who made all men live on that day of completing the Sacred Eye in Heliopolis."[51]

The deceased greeted Osiris in this way and, in so doing, began what was known as the "negative confession," or profession of innocence. After that, the deceased had to turn to the 42 Assessors of Maat, each of which had a descriptive name and demanded a specific confession, and declare his innocence to each in ritualized form:

> O Far-strider who came forth from Heliopolis, I have done no falsehood.
>
> O Fire-embracer who came forth from Kheraha, I have not robbed.
>
> O Nosey who came forth from Hermopolis, I have not been rapacious.
>
> O Swallower of shades who came forth from the cavern, I have not stolen.
>
> O Dangerous One who came forth from Rosetjau, I have not killed men.

---

[50] ibid.
[51] See Faulkner 2001

O Double Lion who came forth from the sky, I have not destroyed food-supplies.

O Fiery Eyes who came forth from Letopolis, I have done no crookedness.

O Flame which came forth backwards, I have not stolen the god's-offerings.

O Bone-breaker who came forth from Heracleopolis, I have not told lies.

O Green of flame who came forth from Memphis, I have not taken food.[52]

The names of these gods were often different from their original names, but some of them are decipherable. For instance, the "Far-Strider" from Heliopolis is most likely Ra, the sun god, whose home was the city of Heliopolis ("City of the Sun" in Greek). The brilliantly named "Nosey" is probably a reference to Thoth, whose animal form was that of ibis.[53]

After this, the deceased addressed the god of the Hall of Justice and would then be questioned by the 42 gods, who asked about the deceased's name, their travels, and the things they passed on their way to their hall. The gods also asked them what they saw, what they said, and what they received from the inhabitants of the lands they passed through before they are told to walk through the door to the Hall of Justice, whose parts—the eaves, the floor, the door bolt, the hasp, the cross-timbers, and the door itself—each addressed the deceased and tested them, promising not to let them pass unless they knew the correct response to each of their questions. Then, the deceased addressed their own feet, naming them with sacred names before being allowed through the door and being introduced to Thoth, the Dragoman of the Two Lands, to whom the deceased had to report. After this, Anubis brought the deceased to the scales he kept, and there began the judgment in earnest.

The Weighing of the Heart is possibly the most iconic moment in the ancient Egyptian concept of death. It involves the deceased traveling to meet most of the deities, most notably Osiris, Horus, and the great judge Thoth, to convince them of their right to an afterlife of peace and glory. In the story, Anubis is called the "Keeper of the Scales/Balance," and he weighed the heart against the visual representation of truth and justice: the feather of Maat. If the deceased's heart was heavier than the feather, presumably due to the sins and evils performed in his or her lifetime, the heart and soul of the deceased was eaten by the crocodile-headed god, Ammit.

---

[52] ibid.
[53] Tyldesley 2011

An Egyptian depiction of Anubis weighing the heart

A statuette of an Egyptian kneeling before Anubis

The ancient Egyptians did not have an all-knowing, all-powerful god that would punish an attempt on the part of the deceased to withhold or obfuscate the truth. The following is another spell, taken from *The Book of the Dead*, in which the deceased openly warns anybody from trying to "take his heart away" from him: "O you who take away hearts and accuse hearts, who recreate a man's heart (in respect of) what he has done, he is forgetful of himself through what you have done. Hail to you, lords of eternity, founders of everlasting! Do not take [the deceased's] heart with your fingers wherever his heart may be. You shall not raise any matter harmful to him, because as for this heart of [the deceased], his heart belongs to one whose names are great, whose words are mighty, who possesses his members. He sends out his heart which controls his body, his heart is announced to the gods, for [the deceased's] heart is his own, he has power over it, and he will not say what he has done. He himself has power over his members, his heart obeys him, for he is your lord and you are in his body, you shall not turn aside. I command you to ovey me in the realm of the dead, even I, [the deceased], who am vindicated in peace and vindicated in the beautiful West in the domain of eternity."[54]

---

[54] Spell 27 see Faulkner 2001

This would seem a fairly honest declaration of the trust one has in the innocence of one's heart if there was not another spell appearing to flatter and coax the heart against "betraying" its owner:

> "O my heart which I had from my mother. O my heart which I had upon earth, do not rise up against me as a witness in the presence of the Lord of Things; do not speak against me concerning what I have done, do not bring up anything against me in the presence of the Great God, Lord of the West.
>
> "Hail to you, my heart! Hail to you, my heart! Hail to you, my entrails! Hail to you, you gods who are at the head of those who wear the side lock, who lean on their staffs! May you say what is good to Re, may you make me flourish, may powers be bestowed when I go forth, having been interred among the great ones who long endure upon earth.
>
> "Not dying in the West, but becoming a spirit in it."[55]

The reference to the West is a reference to the *Duat*, or Land of the Dead, where the sun set.

The spell that follows this is a wonderful example of the ubiquity of people's fear of death, in which the deceased doubles down on the supplication to their own heart. In this spell, there is also a reassuring response from the gods the deceased was supposed to meet (reassuring, at least, to the priests officiating the dead person's burial). It occurs immediately after Anubis takes the deceased by the hand and presents him or her to the council of gods, who are often depicted as surrounding the scales "kept" by Anubis.

> "O my heart which I had from my mother! O my heart which I had from my mother! O my heart of my different ages! Do not stand up as a witness against me, do not be opposed to me in the tribunal, do not be hostile to me in the presence of the Keeper of the Balance, for you are my ka which was in my body, the protector who made my members hale. Go forth to the happy place whereto we speed; do not make my name stink to the Entourage who make men. Do not tell lies about me in the presence of the god; it is indeed well that you should hear!
>
> "Thus says Thoth, judge of truth, to the Great Ennead which is in the presence of Osiris: Hear this word of very truth. I have judged the heart of the deceased, and his soul stands as a witness for him. His deeds are righteous in the great balance, and no sin has been found in him. He did not diminish the offerings in the temples, he did not destroy what had been made, he did not go about with deceitful speech while he was on earth.

---

[55] Spell 30a see Faulkner 2001

"Thus says the Great Ennead to Thoth who is in Hermopolis: This utterance of yours is true. The vindicated Osiris [name of the deceased here, associating him with the god of the dead] is straightforward, he has no sin, there is no accusation against him before us, Ammit shall not be permitted to have power oer him. Let there be given to him the offerings which are issued in the presence of Osiris, and may a grant of land be established in the Field of Offerings as for the Followers of Horus.

"Thus says Horus son of Isis: I have come to you, O Wennefer, and I bring [the deceased] to you. His heart is true, having gone forth from the balance, and he has not sinned against any god or any goddess. Thoth has judged him in writing which has been told to the Ennead, and Maat the great has witnessed. Le there be given to him bread and he will be for ever like the followers of Horus.

"Thus says [the deceased]: Here I am in your presence, O Lord of the West. There is no wrong-doing in my body, I have no wittingly told lies, there has been no second fault. Grant that I may be like the favoured ones who are in your suite, O Osiris, one greatly favoured by the good god, one loved of the Lord of the Two Lands, [the deceased] vindicated before Osiris."[56]

One ancient artifact found by archeologists was a "heart scarab" amulet with Spell 30 (a or b) inscribed on it. It was inserted in the mummy wrappings to ensure the deceased's heart would stay true to its owner.[57] Rather than a reassuring episode, however, this text gives a basic checklist of what not to do in life.

For many years, scholars and popular writers have framed *The Book of the Dead* as the "Egyptian Bible,"[58] and although this has since been proven to be a wildly inappropriate comparison, the passage does hint at some of basic tenets of the religion. Respecting the temple, maintaining rather than destroying, and choosing to speak the truth over lies are certainly what the ancient Egyptians (and practically every other religious person since) believed to make a person worthy of an everlasting life of peace and glory, rather than suffer a murky doom in the depths of a crocodile's gullet. It is likely that this text is also an example of sympathetic magic - the scene is depicted by somebody who has already been in the hall of justice and returned to give other humans a verbatim description of what will happen to them. As such, it is a simulacrum of the weighing of the heart, and one that depicts the best possible result, thus serving the same purpose as other examples of sympathetic magic, namely imitation, to turn it into reality.

---

[56] Spell 30B see Faulkner 2001
[57] Tyldesley 2011
[58] Pinch 2002

Truth-Teller

The connection between death and truth is one of the most persistent in mythologies from across the ancient world. There is a recurring theme of the dead being possessors of the truth or able to access otherworldly truth in some way.

For example, there are many accounts of people seeking the "wisdom of the dead" in ancient Greek mythology. The purview of necromancers more than the general populace, the most famous example is Odysseus, who sought the wisdom of the dead prophet Tiresias. There are also a number of magic spells written on lead or stone that are "addressed" to the dead with the hope that the world of the living would somehow benefit from their otherworldly experiences.

In the case of Anubis, thanks to his aforementioned role in the weighing of the heart and the journey of the recently deceased in the Duat, his connection with truth is easy to imagine, at least in his home country. There is even evidence to suggest that his fame spread beyond the borders of Egypt, particularly in connection with the truth. The so-called Rhadamanthine Oath refers to the Cretan King (and later Judge of the Underworld) Rhadamanthus' prohibition of using the gods' actual names when swearing oaths. Instead, he ordered oath-swearers to take symbolic monikers for the gods they swore upon, so instead of "by Zeus" or "in the name of Athena," they would say "by the eagle" or "in the name of the owl."

The custom spread to Athens where it became commonplace for the legendary philosopher Socrates. In his writings, Plato recorded Socrates uttering the oath "in the name of the dog" or "by the dog" on many occasions. One such occasion is in Plato's *Phaedrus*, in which Socrates discusses love and rhetoric with his young aristocratic friend, Phaedrus. In a moment of brilliance, Socrates sees through Phaedrus' false humility and timidity when the young man asks how Socrates can believe he has learned the eloquent speech of Lysius. Referring to himself as "the man who is sick with the love of discourse," Socrates urges Phaedrus to get on with his retelling of Lysius' speech: "O Phaedrus! If I don't know Phaedrus, I have forgotten myself. But since neither of these things is true, I know very well that when listening to Lysias, he did not hear once only, but often urged him to repeat; and he gladly obeyed. Yet even that was not enough for Phaedrus, but at last he borrowed the book and read what he especially wished, and doing this he sat from early morning. Then, when he grew tired, he went for a walk, with the speech, as I believe, by the Dog, learned by heart, unless it was very long. And he was going outside the wall to practice it. And meeting the man who is sick with the love of discourse, he was glad when he saw him, because he would have someone to share his revel, and told him to lead on. But when the lover of discourse asked him to speak, he feigned coyness, as if he did not yearn to speak; at last, however, even if no one would listen willingly, he was bound to speak whether or no. So, Phaedrus, ask him to do now what he will presently do anyway."[59]

---

[59] Phaedr. 228b, see Fowler 1925

Socrates uses the oath as more than an exclamation of exasperation when speaking to a young man he knows wishes to talk about love but deliberates too much. In Plato's *Gorgias*,[60] Socrates uses it to deliberate on the existence of a "perfect knowledge" that somehow transcends the fickleness and corruption of rhetoric and rhetoricians. Later on in the dialogue,[61] Socrates says, "[Rhetoric] seems to me then, Gorgias, to be a pursuit that is not a matter of art, but showing a shrewd, gallant spirit which has a natural bent for clever dealing with mankind, and I sum up its substance in the name flattery. [Whereas Philosophy,] my dear friend, speaks what you hear me saying now, and she is far less fickle to me than any other favourite: that son of Cleinias is ever changing his views, but philosophy always holds the same, and it is her speech that now surprises you, and she spoke it in your own presence. So you must either refute her, as I said just now, by proving that wrongdoing and impunity for wrong done is not the uttermost evil; or, if you leave that unproved, by the Dog, god of the Egyptians, there will be no agreement between you, Callicles, and Callicles, but you will be in discord with him all your life. And yet I, my very good sir, should rather choose to have my lyre, or some chorus that I might provide for the public, out of tune and discordant, or to have any number of people disagreeing with me and contradicting me, than that I should have internal discord and contradiction in my own single self."62

Socrates was eventually killed for his beliefs and teachings, and according to Plato, he had the chance to escape punishment but chose not to. In Plato's *Apology*, Socrates explains how he defended himself against the charges and how his defense made his accusers hate him even more:

> "So examining this man—for I need not call him by name, but it was one of the
> public men with regard to whom I had this kind of experience, men of Athens—and
> conversing with him, this man seemed to me to seem to be wise to many other
> people and especially to himself, but not to be so; and then I tried to show him that
> he thought he was wise, but was not. As a result, I became hateful to him and to
> many of those present; and so, as I went away, I thought to myself, "I am wiser than
> this man; for neither of us really knows anything fine and good, but this man thinks
> he knows something when he does not, whereas I, as I do not know anything, do not
> think I do either. I seem, then, in just this little thing to be wiser than this man at
> any rate, that what I do not know I do not think I know either." From him I went to
> another of those who were reputed to be wiser than he, and these same things
> seemed to me to be true; and there I became hateful both to him and to many others.
>
> "After this then I went on from one to another, perceiving that I was hated, and
> grieving and fearing, but nevertheless I thought I must consider the god's business

---

60 466c
61 463a
62 482B

of the highest importance. So I had to go, investigating the meaning of the oracle, to all those who were reputed to know anything. <u>And by the Dog</u>, men of Athens—for I must speak the truth to you—this, I do declare, was my experience: those who had the most reputation seemed to me to be almost the most deficient, as I investigated at the god's behest, and others who were of less repute seemed to be superior men in the matter of being sensible."[63]

Again, this initially appears to be a simple exclamation, but in the context of the charges against Socrates (one of which was "refusing to recognize the gods of the state"), his use of a Rhadamanthine oath to refer to Anubis and none of the other gods is certainly interesting. This is not to say that Socrates was trying to subvert the Greek gods by referring to Egyptian gods, but it's certainly interesting that a philosopher who was known for choosing his words with care would repeatedly use that expression irf place of any other.

Socrates was found guilty of the charges and subsequently condemned to drink a dose of hemlock in his cell. His friends gathered around him to tell him they had friends in high places who could whisk him off to live his years out abroad. In true ancient Greek tragic style, Socrates dampens his friends' hopes, telling them, "For, by the Dog, I fancy these bones and sinews of mine would have been in Megara or Boeotia long ago, carried thither by an opinion of what was best, if I did not think it was better and nobler to endure any penalty the city may inflict rather than to escape and run away."[64]

Why did Socrates use this expression so often? Perhaps the spread of Anubis' cult, or at least his iconic appearance and assumed function, influenced ancient Greek society to such a degree that it simply became a common phrase uttered by many people, similar to how "by Jove" was often used by Shakespeare and continued to be a common minced oath up into the early 20th century. Whatever the reason, the curious connection between Socrates and Anubis is certainly proof of how interconnected the ancient world was.

---

[63] *Apology* 21 C-E
[64] *Phaedo* 98 E

Hermanubis

A hybrid statue combining aspects of Hermes and Anubis

"Hermes is the representative of reason and speech, which both accomplish and interpret all things. The phallic Hermes represents vigour, but also indicates the generative law that pervades all things. Further, reason is composite: in the sun it is called Hermes; in the moon Hecate; and that which is in the All Hermopan, for the generative and creative reason extends over all things. Hermanubis also is composite, and as it were half Greek, being found among the Egyptians also. Since speech is also connected with the power of love, Eros represents this power: wherefore Eros is represented as the son of Hermes, but as an infant, because of his sudden impulses of desire."[65] This quote from the ancient philosopher Porphyry is from his lesser-known treaties *On*

Statues (or *On Religious Images*), and it draws a stark connection between Hermes and Anubis by highlighting the Roman practice of drawing the two gods together.

The name Hermanubis is from the Roman period, but there is at least one reference to this distinct god before the Common Era. What sets Hermanubis apart from many of the other "polytheophoric" figures that combined multiple gods is that Hermanubis was considered a god in his own right.

Hermes is traditionally associated with the Egyptian god, Thoth, the god of writing and magic, but in the case of Anubis, the connection is derived from both gods' roles as psychopomp. Nevertheless, the character of Hermanubis (as far as it can be drawn from surviving texts) has a hue more mystical than Hermes or Anubis on their own. Plutarch associated Hermanubis with the same duality of "things above" and "things below," writing that "the relation which discloses the things in the heavens and belongs to the things which tend upward is sometimes named Anubis and sometimes Hermanubis as belonging in part to the things above and in part to the things below. For this reason they sacrifice to him on the one hand a white cock and on the other hand one of saffron color, regarding the former things as simple and clear, and the others as combined and variable."[66]

As already mentioned, elsewhere in Plutarch's writings, he described Anubis' duality in this respect as coming from his being the son of "dual mothers," Isis and Nephthys. Isis was associated with "mysteries," those secretive religious orders or festivals increasingly common across the Mediterranean, perhaps most famously at Eleusinia, the details of which are still a mystery.

Apuleius highlighted Isis' mysterious nature in his famous work, *The Golden Ass*, in which he tells the story of a man obsessed with magic who accidentally turns himself into an ass instead of a bird, which was his original intention. The man, Lucius, wanders the world trying to find redemption or salvation until he finally appeals to the great "Mother of the Universe." This "mother" is exactly the kind of goddess Plutarch tried to extrapolate from his studies of religions in the Mediterranean:

"I come, Lucius, moved by your entreaties: I, mother of the universe, mistress of all the elements, first-born of the ages, highest of the gods, queen of the shades, first of those who dwell in heaven, representing in one shape all gods and goddesses. My will controls the shining heights of heaven, the health-giving sea-winds, and the mournful silences of hell; the entire world worships my single godhead in a thousand shapes, with diverse rites, and under many a different name. The Phrygians, first-born of mankind, call me the Pessinuntian Mother of the gods; the native Athenians the Cecropian Minerva; the island-dwelling Cypriots Paphian Venus; the archer

---

[65] Porphyry *De Imaginibus*
[66] *On Isis and Osiris 61*

Cretans Dictynnan Diana; the triple-tongued Sicilians Stygian Proserpine; the ancient Eleusinians Actaean Ceres; some call me Juno, some Bellona, others Hecate, others Rhamnusia; but both races of Ethiopians, those on whom the rising and those on whom the setting sun shines, and the Egyptians who excel in ancient learning, honour me with the worship which is truly mine and call me by my true name: Queen Isis. I am here in pity for your misfortunes, I am here with favour and goodwill. Cease now your weeping, put an end to your lamentation, banish your grief: now by my Providence the day of your release is dawning. Attend therefore with your whole mind to the orders I give you.

"The day which will be born of this night has been consecrated to me by immemorial religious usage. It is the day on which the tempests of winter have abated and the stormy sea-waves have subsided, when the ocean is again navigable and my priests sacrifice a brand-new ship as the first offering of the season's trade. It is this ceremony that you must await without anxiety and without unholy thoughts. My priest has been warned by me; he will be carrying in his right hand as part of his processional equipment a sistrum wreathed with a garland of roses. You must not hesitate, but make your way briskly through the crowd and join the procession, relying on my goodwill. Approach the priest and, as if kissing his hand, gently take a bite of the roses, and in a moment you will divest yourself of the hide of this vile beast that has always been so hateful to me. Do not fear that anything I tell you to do will be difficult. At the very moment that I am appearing to you, I am also present to my priest while he sleeps, telling him what must be done next. At my orders the serried ranks of the crowd will give you passage, and amid the joyful ceremonies and festive spectacles no one will be repelled by that ugly appearance you wear or put a sinister construction on your sudden change of shape and make spiteful accusations against you.

"But this you must remember well and keep forever stored up in your inmost heart: the remaining course of your life right up until your last breath is now solemnly promised to me. It is only just that you should make over all the rest of your time on earth to her by whose beneficence you will be made human again. And you will live happily, you will live gloriously under my protection; and when you have completed your lifespan and descend to the shades, there also in that subterranean hemisphere I, whom you now behold, shall be there, shining amidst the darkness of Acheron and reigning in the secret depths of Styx, and you shall dwell in the Elysian Fields and constantly worship me and be favoured by me. But if by diligent observance and pious service and steadfast chastity you shall have deserved well of my godhead, know that I alone also have the power to prolong your life beyond the bounds fixed for you by your Fate."

"The awesome prophecy was ended, and the invincible goddess withdrew into herself. I at once awoke from sleep and arose with mixed feelings of fear and joy, followed by a mighty sweat. Greatly wondering at the way in which the powerful goddess had manifested herself to my sight, I bathed in the sea and, attentive to her august commands, began to con over her instructions point by point...

"Then came the throng of those initiated in the mysteries, men and women of all ranks and ages in shining robes of pure white linen. The women's hair was perfumed and covered with a transparent veil, the men had their heads clean-shaven and gleaming, and their sistrums of bronze or silver or in some cases gold combined to produce a clear shrill strain. There followed the earthly stars of the great faith, the priests of the cult, those grandees, clad in tightly-fitting white linen from breast to ankle and displaying the symbols of the most mighty gods in all their glory. The first held up a lamp burning with a bright flame, not one like those which light our dinner-tables at night, but a boat-shaped vessel of gold feeding a more ample flame from its central opening. The second was similarly attired, but carried in both hands one of those altars called Altars of Succour, so named from the succouring Providence of the sovereign goddess. A third came bearing aloft a golden palm-branch of delicate workmanship and a copy of Mercury's caduceus. A fourth displayed an image of Justice, a model of a left hand with palm outstretched: this hand, as naturally inactive and unendowed with cleverness or contrivance, being thought more apt to symbolize justice than the right. He was also carrying a gold vessel rounded in the shape of a breast from which he poured libations of milk. A fifth carried a golden basket heaped with laurel branches, and a sixth a large jar.

"Next appeared the gods who deigned to proceed on human feet. First was the dread messenger between the gods above and the Underworld, his dog's head held high aloft, his face now black, now gold: Anubis, holding a caduceus in his right hand and brandishing a green palm-leaf in his left. Hard on his heels followed a cow standing upright, the fertile image of the All-Mother, proudly borne on the shoulders of one of her blessed priests. Another was carrying a chest containing mystic emblems and securely concealing the secrets of the glorious faith. Another carried in his fortunate embrace the worshipful image of the supreme divinity."[67]

The notion of an "All-Mother" was beginning to gain popularity, as was Isis' cult, across the Roman Empire during Apuleius' lifetime. This coincided with many new syncretic religions and composite lines of thought, such as Neo-Platonism, Gnosticism, and Hermeticism. Also called "Hermetic Philosophy," this is the modern term for what is known as the Corpus Hermeticum, a body of work unifying many tenets of ancient Greek, Egyptian, Middle Eastern, and Christian

---

[67] *The Golden Ass Book 11* see Kenny's excellent translation (1998)

philosophy and religion into a more esoteric line of thought. It can be easily inferred from the name that Hermes is the predominant force in this philosophy, but it is not the Hermes worshiped by the ancient Greeks. This was a reference to Hermes Trismegistus, often known as "Thrice-Great Hermes," who was an amalgamation of Hermes and Thoth. Later authors came to believe was a great, pre-Christian man who wrote most of the Corpus Hermeticum, but that belief was disproved just after the Renaissance.

The first time his name appears is in a rare text known as the *Emerald Tablet*, dated to Arab sources in the 8th-9th centuries CE, and he is mentioned as the author of an interesting quote earlier associated with Hermanubis:

> "Tis true without lying, certain & most true.
> That which is below is like that which is above & that which is above is like that which is below to do the miracles of one only thing
> And as all things have been & arose from one by the mediation of one: so all things have their birth from this one thing by adaptation.
> The Sun is its father, the moon its mother, the wind hath carried it in its belly, the earth is its nurse.
> The father of all perfection in the whole world is here.
> Its force or power is entire if it be converted into earth.
> Separate thou the earth from the fire, the subtle from the gross sweetly with great industry.
> It ascends from the earth to the heaven & again it descends to the earth & receives the force of things superior & inferior.
> By this means you shall have the glory of the whole world
> & thereby all obscurity shall fly from you.
> Its force is above all force. For it vanquishes every subtle thing & penetrates every solid thing.
> So was the world created.
> From this are & do come admirable adaptations whereof the means (or process) is here in this. Hence I am called Hermes Trismegist, having the three parts of the philosophy of the whole world
> That which I have said of the operation of the Sun is accomplished & ended."

"That which is below is like that which is above" is a quote reminiscent of Plutarch's story of Anubis' two mothers (Isis above, Nephthys below), and it influenced alchemists well into the 18th century. In fact, the above translation came from none other than Sir Isaac Newton, who practiced alchemy.

In a way, this is Anubis' lasting legacy. Just as he had once held the mysterious position of "king of the dead," he later rose to prominence as the mysterious being of above and below.

Though the Emerald Tablet does not mention Anubis directly, it is most certainly of the dog-god's ilk. The Emerald Tablet was long held to be a cryptic recipe or formula for making the Philosopher's Stone, the epitome of the alchemical process, promising eternal life. The same promise was offered by the priests of Anubis, who mixed unguents and followed mysterious ritualistic practices in the mummification of the deceased.

Despite the fact that Anubis does not make many appearances in the main myths of the ancient Egyptians, his importance is in no way diminished. Given the importance of the king and kingship in general, figures like Osiris, Horus, and Seth all rise above the rest since theirs is a story of battling for the throne, rather than achieving immortality. However, when ancient Egyptians looked upon a graveyard and watched wolves stalking the lands that would one day be their final resting places, it was Anubis whom they considered when their journeys into the next life - whatever that might be – preoccupied their thoughts.

Online Resources

Other books about Egypt by Charles River Editors

Other books about ancient history by Charles River Editors

Other books about Anubis on Amazon

Bibliography

Assmann, J., (1995) *Egyptian Solar Religion in the new Kingdom: Re, Amun, and the Crisis of Polytheism* Translated by A. Alcock, London

Babbitt, F. C., (1936) *Plutarch's Moralia & On Isis and Osiris* Loeb Classical Library

Bowie, F., (2007) *The Anthropology of Religion, An Introduction* Blackwell

Campbell, J. (2008) *The Hero With A Thousand Faces* University of Princeton

Faulkner, R. O., (2001) *The Ancient Egyptian Book of the Dead* The British Museum Press

Fowler, H., (1925) *Plato: Volume 9* Harvard University Press

Frazer, J. G., (1922) *The Golden Bough* Macmillan

Fronthingham, A. L., (1916) *Babylonian Origin of Hermes the Snake-God, and of the Caduceus* American Journal of Archaeology Vo. 20, No. 2 (Apr. – Jun.) pp.175 - 211

Graves, R., (1955) *The Greek Myths* Penguin

Griffiths, J. G., (1980) *The Origins of Osiris and his Cult* E. J. Brill

Hornung, E., (1990) *The Valley of the Kings: Horizon of Eternity* Translated by D. Warburton, New York

Hamilton Gifford, E., (Trans. 1903) *Praeparatio Evangelica by Eusebius* Typographeo Academico

Hyde, L., (2008) *Trickster Makes This World: How Disruptive Imagination Creates Culture* Canongate Books

Kenny, E. J., [trans] (1998) *Apuleis' The Golden Ass* Penguin Classics

Kirk, G. S., (1996) *Myth: Its Meaning And Function In Ancient And Other Cultures* California

King, C. W., (1908) *Plutarch's Morals: Theosophical Essays* London

Mercer, S., (1952) *The Pyramid Texts* Longman's, Green & Co.

Meyer. M. W., (1987) *The Ancient Mysteries: A Sourcebook* Harper Collins

Oldfather, C. H., (1939) *Diodorus Siculus: The Library of History* Loeb Classical Library

Pinch, G., (2002) *Egyptian Mythology: A Guide to the Gods, Goddesses, and Traditions of Ancient Egypt* Oxford University Press

Plutarch. *Plutarch's Lives.* trans. Bernadotte Perrin. Cambridge, MA. Harvard University Press.

Quirke, S., (2001) *The Cult of Ra Sun Worship in Ancient Egypt* London

Roberts, A., & Donaldson, J., (trans.) (1885) *The Anti-Nicene Fathers Volume II* Edinburgh

Shaw, G. J., (2015) *The Egyptian Myths: A Guide to the Ancient Gods and Legends* Thames & Hudson Ltd. London

Simpson, W. K., (1972) *The Literature of Ancient Egypt* Yale University Press

Tyldesley, J., (2011) *The Penguin Book of Myths & Legends of Ancient Egypt* Penguin Books

Tyldesley, J., (2004) *Pyramids: The Real Story Behind Egypt's Most Ancient Monuments* Penguin Books

Wallis Budge, E. A. (1912) *Legends of the Gods: The Egyptian Texts* London

Zandee, Jan., (1960) *Death as an Enemy: According to Ancient Egyptian Conceptions* Brill

Archive

Free Books by Charles River Editors

We have brand new titles available for free most days of the week. To see which of our titles are currently free, click on this link.

Discounted Books by Charles River Editors

We have titles at a discount price of just 99 cents everyday. To see which of our titles are currently 99 cents, click on this link.

Made in the USA
Las Vegas, NV
17 February 2022

44129522R00031